Barbara Hume

ANGEL CHILD

by Val Teal
Pictures by Pelagie Doane

RAND McNALLY & COMPANY

· CHICAGO ·

One day some angels were playing on a cloud.
There were big angels and little angels and one
who was only a baby.

The big angels kept saying, "Now stay right here on this big white cloud. Those small dark ones have rain in them, and if you get on them you'll get your wings wet."

The baby angel thought he'd like to see the rain, so he wandered to the edge of the big white cloud and peeped over. He leaned over too far!

He would have fallen if it hadn't been for his wings. But his wings let him fly quietly to one of the small dark clouds.

He landed on it gently and didn't get his wings wet at all. So he stayed there and sailed along on the little black cloud.

It was fun to be alone. The cloud flew down low and the baby angel could see the sights on the earth below.

But then the cloud flew lower and suddenly, before he knew it, the baby angel dropped—*smack!*—into a tree. The cloud burst, and the rain went everywhere, especially on the baby angel's wings.

He couldn't fly one bit with heavy, wet wings, and besides, his beautiful blue robe was caught on a branch.

He started to cry.

Peter and Patty were playing beneath the tree. When they felt the rain and heard the crying, they looked up.

They were a little surprised to see an angel caught in their tree. They felt sorry for him.

"We'll get you down," they called.

So they ran to Peter's mother, who was lying down with a cold cloth on her head.

"There's a baby angel caught in our tree," they said. "Come and get him down."

But Peter's mother said, "Run along, please, and don't bother me. I have *such* a headache."

Then they went to Patty's mother, but she was having a party and wouldn't listen.

So they got a ladder. And Patty held it while Peter went up and pulled the baby angel off the branch and backed down with him.

The baby angel's robe was all torn, and Peter and Patty wondered what they should do about it. It didn't look nice at all, the way the angel showed through.

Patty said, "Have you got a safety pin, Peter?"

Peter had one where the button was gone from the side of his suit. So he unpinned it.

Peter pinned up the baby angel's torn robe while Patty comforted him. She said, "Don't cry, Angel Child."

So he didn't cry.

"What shall we do with him?" Peter said.

And Patty said, "We'll give him to your mother. She wants a baby. She said she might get one in the fall."

But Peter said, "I don't know if she'll like one with wings."

"We'll put one of your sleepers on him," Patty said, "and that will cover up his wings."

"But what about baths?" Peter said.

And Patty said, "By bath time your mother will be so fond of him that she won't mind his wings."

They took Angel Child in through the kitchen and up the back stairs. Magnolia, the cook, was so surprised that she spilled the pudding she was making.

Peter and Patty put a sleeper on Angel Child and got his wings inside, but they made a hump.

They put him in the crib Peter's mother had ready for the baby she might get in the fall.

But Angel Child didn't want to lie in a bed with his wings buttoned in. He cried and cried.

Peter and Patty were afraid he might wake Peter's mother, so they took him out of bed.

They decided they would have to get him good and sleepy first.

They knew that baths make people sleepy, so they put Angel Child into the bathtub. They ran warm water on him and washed him good all over, his wings too.

Peter's mother heard them. She called down to Magnolia, "What *are* those children doing?"

And Magnolia said, "They're doing no harm, the darlings. Those blessed children are getting better every day."

When Peter and Patty got Angel Child all dry except his wings, which were hard to dry, they put his robe back on him.

They went outdoors and played hide-and-go-seek, but Angel Child didn't know how to play. When they couldn't find him, he'd come out and help them look. So that was no fun.

Then they put him in the swing and pushed him. And Angel Child liked that so much that he did not want to get out when it was Patty's turn.

So, because he was little, they kept on swinging him. And all the time Angel Child's wings kept getting drier and drier.

Pretty soon he unfolded them, and then how high he did swing! He fluttered his wings and went way up.

Then he folded his wings and went way back. And then he fluttered them and went way up, even higher.

And pretty soon he went so high that he went right over the top of the swing.

The rope twisted around the pole and broke!

But Angel Child didn't fall. He kept right on going, because his wings were all dry.

And the last Peter and Patty saw of him, he was flying straight up, still holding on to the seat of the swing.

Peter's father thought some big boys must have broken the swing.

And Peter and Patty felt very sad because Angel Child was gone.

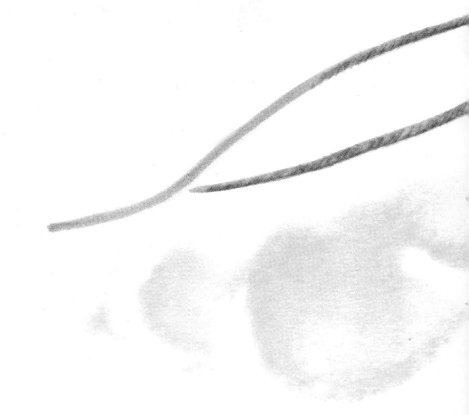